the **Animániacs** in

Sir Yaksalot and the Dragon

Adapted by Matthew Lewis
Based on a television script by Paul Rugg
Drawings by Tony Cervone

TM

FAMILY ENTERTAINMENT

READING

SCHOLASTIC INC.
New York   Toronto   London   Auckland   Sydney

Cover illustration: Erik Doescher
Penciller: Tony Cervone
Inker: Mike DeCarlo
Art Direction and Design: Neuwirth & Associates, Inc.

ISBN 0-590-53531-5

ANIMANIACS, characters, names, and all related indicia are trademarks of Warner Bros. © 1996.
All rights reserved. Published by Scholastic Inc.

12 11 10 9 8 7 6 5 4 3 2 1   6 7 8 9/9 0 1/0

Printed in the U.S.A.   40
First Scholastic printing, September 1996

CHAPTER 1

DRAG IN THE DRAGON

CAMELOT! THE MOST CELEBRATED
KINGDOM IN THE HISTORY OF BRITAIN,

4

7

8

9

15

16

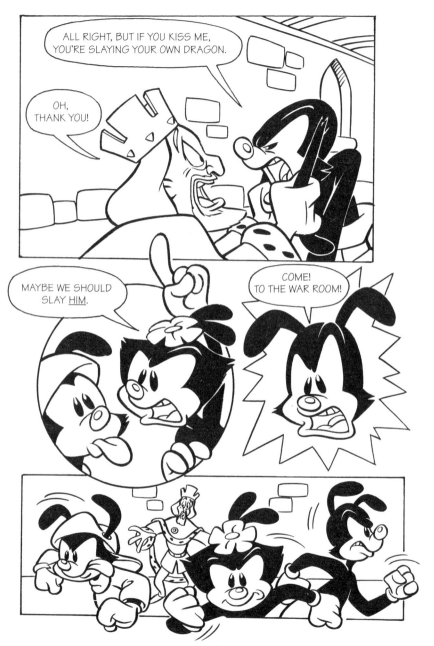

27

28

29

31

HEY, HOW ABOUT THAT LADY IN THE LAKE? I MEAN, SINCE WHEN IS SWORD FIGHTING A WATER SPORT?

CANDY? GUM? DYNAMITE?

37

BOOM! CRASH!

44

45

SMOOSH!

47

49

50

CHAPTER 3

GUESS WHO'S BACK!

TA-DA!

IF WE SLEW THE DRAGON, THEN WHO'S THAT?

THE SCALY GREEN POWER RANGER?

WHAT I SAID ABOUT NOT NEEDING YOU BEFORE...I'D LIKE TO CHANGE MY MIND, IF I COULD.

DON'T GO CHANGING TO TRY TO PLEASE LITTLE OL' ME...

58

64

67

71

CHAPTER 4

DUNGEONS
AND
DRAGONS

73

79

81

84

86

88

89